True Ghost Stories

True Ghost Stories Of Terrifying Paranormal Activity, Haunted Houses And Spooky Places From Around The World

Jo Lavine

© **Copyright 2015 by Jo Lavine - All rights reserved.**

This document is geared towards providing exact and reliable information in regards to the topic and issue covered. The publication is sold with the idea that the publisher is not required to render accounting, officially permitted, or otherwise, qualified services. If advice is necessary, legal or professional, a practiced individual in the profession should be ordered.

- From a Declaration of Principles which was accepted and approved equally by a Committee of the American Bar Association and a Committee of Publishers and Associations.

In no way is it legal to reproduce, duplicate, or transmit any part of this document in either electronic means or in printed format. Recording of this publication is strictly prohibited and any storage of this document is not allowed unless with written permission from the publisher. All rights reserved.

The information provided herein is stated to be truthful and consistent, in that any liability, in terms of

True Ghost Stories

inattention or otherwise, by any usage or abuse of any policies, processes, or directions contained within is the solitary and utter responsibility of the recipient reader. Under no circumstances will any legal responsibility or blame be held against the publisher for any reparation, damages, or monetary loss due to the information herein, either directly or indirectly.

Respective authors own all copyrights not held by the publisher.

The information herein is offered for informational purposes solely, and is universal as so. The presentation of the information is without contract or any type of guarantee assurance.

The trademarks that are used are without any consent, and the publication of the trademark is without permission or backing by the trademark owner. All trademarks and brands within this book are for clarifying purposes only and are the owned by the owners themselves, not affiliated with this document.

Cover image courtesy of Karen - Flickr - https://www.flickr.com/photos/56832361@N00/1717471664/

Jo Lavine

Table of Contents

Introduction	vi
Chapter 1: Most Harmful Poltergeist Cases	1
Chapter 2 : Dolls That Haunt	13
Chapter 3 : Horror Movies That Were Based On Real Life Events	19
Chapter 4 : Spookiest Places Around The World	24
Chapter 5 : Most Unexplained Paranormal Activities	37
Chapter 6 : World's Most Famous Haunted Items	42
Chapter 7 : World's Most Famous Ghosts	51
Chapter 8 : Scary Ghost Towns	55
Chapter 9 : Bizarre Creatures	73
Chapter 10 : Hotel Mysteries	82
Conclusion	92

True Ghost Stories

Do you want more books?

How would you like books arriving in your inbox each week?

Don't worry they are FREE!

We publish books on all sorts of non-fiction niches and send them out to our subscribers each week to spread the love.

All you have to do is sign up and you're good to go!

Just go to the link at the end of this book, sign up, sit back and wait for your book downloads to arrive!

We couldn't have made it any easier! Enjoy!

Jo Lavine

Introduction

Did you ever own a doll or unusual object? Did you feel anything strange about it?

Have you dared yourself to visit a haunted house, or a spooky place? If someone sells a "haunted" item in an online selling store, would you buy it? Should an item decide your death by using it... will you still use it? What movies were based on true horror stories?

In this book you will read about the worlds' scariest stories about ghosts, haunted places, items that you should never bring home, dolls that haunt, and the most unexplained paranormal activities.

It is up to you if you believe them or not.

Whatever is your reason for reading this book, be certain that you love the thrill, because the contents are not for the frail of heart. The time of the day you will read it is of course you choice. But night time when the lights are off would be the most challenging!

Thanks again for purchasing this book, I hope you enjoy it!

Are you ready? Then turn to the next page...

Chapter 1: Most Harmful Poltergeist Cases

Poltergeists are ghosts that are capable of hurting you. They can move things and throw objects if they want to. Unfortunately, poltergeists are hateful entities… so more often than not, they would always want to hurt anyone who comes their way. Their name, which is of German origin, translates into "Noisy Ghosts". Very fitting, don't you think?

In this section, you will learn about the most terrifying Poltergeist cases ever recorded.

1. The Angry Mckenzie Ghosts in Greyfriars Cemetery

Before anything else, let's get a clear picture of who George McKenzie was. McKenzie was a lawyer back in the 1600s. During his time, King Charles II wanted a group of Presbyterians (called Covenanters) to change their religions. When the group refused to follow the King's commands, McKenzie signed their persecution papers. Some of them were executed, but many were also imprisoned.

The prison (now called Covenanters Prison), had veryinhumane methods back then. Most of the prisoners would be left with little food, and subjected to the cold winters without any form of heat, and if they were not killed, they were sold to become slaves.

The funny thing is this: when Bloody McKenzie died, he was buried in Greyfriar's Cemetery, which is very close to the Covenanters Prison. His final resting place is now famous in the name of Black Mausoleum and is home to a lot of Poltergeist activities.

It all started in 1999, with a man so homeless that he desperately sought the comforts of cemetery warmth. How wrong could he be because he encountered, not protection, but a hateful spirit.

Reportedly, he climbed into a coffin (in the tomb of George McKenzie, a lawyer who signed the deaths of over 18,000 enemies of the former King Charles II), but instead of being as steady as a rock, the coffin shook on its own... covering the man with dust from the dead.

According to reports, a guard saw the whole commotion and both him and the homeless man were terrified. This incident happened in 1998, and since then, Bloody McKenzie became famous for causing bruises and scratch marks among tourists and grave visitors.

A dog walker saw the event and although he was terrified, he just thought that the man simply saw a ghost. Well, not exactly, because the real disturbances from angry ghosts are yet to come.

From then on people claimed that strange activities kept on happening. In fact it was so bad that the city council had to close the cemetery to the public. It was only when, Jan Andrew Henderson (a historian and a book writer) established a ghost tour that people came to see the cemetery again.

Even Henderson admitted that the case of the McKenzie Poltergeist is uncommon. A poltergeist attack typically happens for a few weeks straight and then it will subside, it also usually targets just one person, or one family.

McKenzie's case went on and on since 1998 (although there were times when no activities were recorded), and it had targeted a lot of people, particularly participants of the Cemetery Tours.

That, also, did not turn out well.

350 of the people who participated in the tour claimed that they had been attacked by unknown forces. 170 of them passed out and a lot also got injuries... including fractured bones!

Should you be around the area of Edinburgh, would you dare visit the cemetery? Or perhaps you may join the tour? While in there, remember that other spirits may be lingering, the Covenanters Prison, after all, is home to tortured spirits.

2. The Poltergeist who loves toys

For their privacy, the names of the victims were not revealed, but through the reports, they were referred to as Marc and Marianne. They were a couple, who were attacked in their home in South Shields... by a poltergeist. What made things more complicated is the fact that they have a three-year old son.

The horror began in 2005, when typical poltergeist activities occurred in their home - doors slamming, cabinets suddenly opening and closing, and items around the house moving around. Their first shocking experience was when they came home to two chairs stacked together on top of the table.

From there, the months became plagued with annoying and puzzling events. Doors would slam without human interference and items would go missing and would reappear in different rooms. What they did not expect though, was when the poltergeist used their son's toys.

One night, Marianne woke up to a dog toy that hit her on the head. She turned on the lights, and guess what? A second toy was staring at her, ready to attack. Helpless, all they did was stoop down for cover under their very fragile duvet.

Through it all, they felt that someone was trying to pull the blanket away. They were able to keep it, but it does not mean that they were untouched, particularly Marc, because he suddenly screamed out in pain. The reason? 13 scratches in his back.

The scratches, however, were gone by the morning.

Finally, Hallowell and Ritson, two famous paranormal experts, decided to take on the case. Since the start of their investigation, they have witnessed almost everything the poltergeist did.

If you think that the ordeal was over, you're very wrong. The poltergeist continued on its attack and it certainly developed a penchant for using toys. Once, they saw a stuffed toy holding a cutter and then the toy horse hanging from the ceiling. Sometimes there were even scary notes left on Robert's blackboard.

And believe it or not, but the poltergeist was even able to send text messages to Marianne's phone! If you are wondering what the text messages contained, well, they are not friendly to say the least.

One said "I'm going to get you bitch" and the other one said "You are dead." When investigated, it turned out that the number where it came from cannot be found on earth; neither a computer nor a mobile phone sent those messages.

As the months went by, the activities also became more malevolent. Marc would often be a victim of large scratches in the middle of his body, and take note, these scratches were seen to vanish right in front of the witnesses' eyes! Ritson and Hallowell saw cupboards being opened, lampshades being swayed and blankets on the bed being moved.

What's even more terrifying is sometimes, the couple could not find their own son. He would be found under the tables and inside the closet where he often clutched his blanket tightly.

On one occasion, he was seen lying on the floor with a plastic table on top of him. He appeared awake because his eyes were open but he was not moving, as if he was under a trance.

The investigators first thought that the activities were only created by repressed emotions, but later on, they doubted it. It is clear that whoever was plaguing the family was a malevolent soul who wanted to bring out fear.

They concluded that this poltergeist actually fed on people's fear, hence the reason why there was no actual harm done, only events that would scare off the couple and their son.

One of the highlights of this case is the water bottle photographed by Ritson and Hallowell. The bottle was on top of the table and was positioned diagonally-- perfectly balanced even when no one was holding it.

Fed up with everything, Marc and Marianne moved out of the house. Ritson and Hallowell, clearly engrossed with the case, wrote a full book about it

3. Esther's Poltergeist

Having a stalker is scary enough, but what would you do if said stalker was a poltergeist?

Well, Esther Cox did not know the answer to that question either. She also did not know why that poltergeist took a liking to her. Said entity followed her to torment her so much that many people witnessed her sufferings. Her case eventually became one of the most famous poltergeist cases in Canadian history.

Her nightmare began while she was residing in the home of her sister. Olive Teed, together with her husband Daniel Teed. Olive and Daniel had two small children. Also living in the house was two of Esther's siblings and Daniel's little brother. But even though their house was already crowded, they still took a boarder named Walter Hubbel, an actor who would later write a book regarding Esther's case.

According to reports, Esther was nearly raped by a shoemaker named Bob MacNeal. Bob was Esther's acquaintance only because she did not know of his bad reputation. She escaped the attack, but it's as if her terror opened up the doors to a more terrifying experience that would follow her with persistence.

On to the story: One night while sleeping, Esther and her little sister, Jennie felt something crawling beneath their bed, and this something was first thought of as a rodent: a simple, harmless rat. The whole house searched for the rodent, but they couldn't find anything.

While sleeping, she felt something crawling beneath her bed, and this something was first thought of as a rodent: a simple, harmless rat.

Night after night, Esther would complain of it, and the whole household would search for the menacing rat. They could not find anything. On one occasion, Esther woke up screaming, and when family members went to the rescue, they saw that the bed was haphazardly unmade. At first they thought that Esther was only imagining things, what with all the stress of being a victim of attempted rape, but what they would witness later would change their minds.

One night, after dinner, Esther told her family that she would be going to bed early because she felt feverish. After some time, Jennie followed her and was surprised when, upon reaching the bed, Esther shouted: "My God, what's happening to me? I feel like I am dying!"

Terrified, Jennie turned on the lights and was shocked to see Esther's whole body swelling. Jennie called their sister Olive and both of them tried to get Esther back to bed and calm her down, but to no avail. It was as if Esther was choking, her skin was bright red, it was swelling, and she was very hot to touch.

Suddenly, four loud bangs were heard from underneath Esther's bed. The bangs were so loud that it shook the whole room. When they looked back at Esther, her skin had returned to normal and she had calmed down enough to send her into a deep, peaceful slumber.

Desperate, they consulted a doctor who watched Esther as she fell asleep. In the middle of the night the same thing happened. The doctor watched as the blankets were pulled and the pillows, thrown.

Another scary thing that happened during that night was when a writing on the wall was initiated using an unknown instrument. The message clearly wrote: "Esther, you are mine to kill!"

Even with the doctor's assistance, Esther was helpless. In fact, the malevolent attacks became more severe. Knives and sharp tools were also hurled and thrown into the woodworks.

Overtime, the cases became even more severe.

The ghost started to create fire and threatened to burn the house, should Esther not leave.

Esther left, but the ghost followed.

Once, when Esther tried to attend a mass, she sat at the rear side of the church. All of a sudden, loud noises could be heard. It was loud and annoying enough to drown out the sermon of the minister. Knowing exactly that she was the cause of the noises, Esther left and the noises also stopped.

She tried to stay with one of their neighbours but when the poltergeist followed her there and started disturbing the innocent family, she also left.

While Esther was working, a knife suddenly flew at her back, injuring her. When a man tried to help, an invisible force grabbed the knife yet again and plunged itself on the same spot at her back. The wound caught infection and Esther almost did not live.

After the ordeal, Esther met a man who had a ridiculous idea. He prompted Esther to "perform" on a stage and let the audience watch as the poltergeist attacked her. Unfortunately, the plan was sabotaged as the ghost seemed not inclined to the idea of performing. People left and Esther and the man were forced to abandon the idea.

After that, Esther started working as a helper, but the ghost was still adamant in making her life hell on earth. The poltergeist caused a fire, and the owners of the house accused Esther of doing it.

Although Esther tried and tried to explain that it was her ghost stalker, she was still charged with arson and was sent to jail.

While in jail, it seemed like the ghost no longer had a penchant for her because the presence diminished until it totally died down. And Esther was left alone by the stalker she did not want in the first place.

Esther was 19 when the attacked first happened and the year it was reported was 1878. After the ordeal Esther was able to marry twice, but she also faced her demise in 1912. After her death, the family's boarder, Walter Hubbel, published his book entitled *The Great Amherst Mystery*.

In the book, 16 people signed affidavits, clearly stating that they were witnesses to the events that happened to Esther.

Chapter 2 : Dolls That Haunt

Dolls are often toys for little girls who want to play mommy. They also serve as nice gifts for people who love dressing up, and doing their hair. What would you do, if the doll that you have, is haunted? What's more, what if this doll is capable of ruining your life?

1. Annabelle

How can someone not mention the story of Annabelle, the haunted doll that has been featured in the movie, The Conjuring, which later on had her own movie?

According to the story, Annabelle was given to Donna by her mother in 1970. At first what the doll did was tolerable: it seemed to be moving on its own, but the movements were just minor – a few position switches here and there.

But as time went by, the movement of the doll became more noticeable, it became bigger. From the bedroom it would transfer to the living room, and beside it would be notes on parchment paper, one note even said "Help me."

What's even more puzzling was the fact that there was not even a single piece of parchment paper in the house.

So, Donna and her room-mate Angie consulted paranormal experts and it was revealed that it was a ghost of an abandoned child. The two of them decided to keep the doll, but another friend named Lou suggested that they should get rid of it. They refused, thinking that doing that would mean leaving a child when she has nowhere to go.

Apparently, the doll too, did not like Lou's suggestion, so he was allegedly attacked by it. After Lou was strangled, Donna and her friend sought out the famous paranormal experts Ed and Lorraine Warren.

Ed and Lorraine confirmed that the doll was indeed possessed, but not by a seven-year old Anabelle Higgins. What held the doll captive was an inhuman demon.

Ed and Lorraine performed an exorcism, and they took the doll with them. The exorcism apparently failed because, on the way home, some mishaps on the road happened, like - their brakes failing.

When the ordeal was over, Annabelle was locked in a museum, and it is said that her encasement is crusted with holy water. She still resides there to this day.

It is said some visitors of the museum have often taunted the doll, and have later experienced near fatal accidents upon leaving the museum.

2. Robert

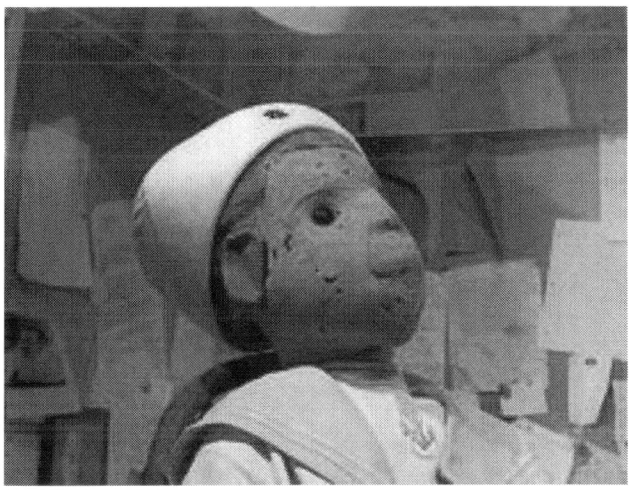

Image Courtesy: Cayobo

In 1906, a very unhappy servant (who was practising black magic) gave Robert Eugene Otto a doll. They named him Robert, taken from the child's first name.

While Eugene had the doll, his parents would often hear him talking to it, and would be surprised to hear the doll talk back. At first, of course, they thought that it was just Eugene and he was just changing his voice.

At the same time, their neighbors often reported that the doll could be seen moving from one window to another. They even swore that the doll was capable of eliciting scary giggles. To make things scarier, even guests would relate that they often saw Robert blink, and that he was also capable of changing his expressions.

Then one night, the whole family awoke to Eugene screaming, and when they entered his room, all the furniture was knocked down. Eugene kept on pointing at the doll and shouting that "Robert did it!"

Amidst all these, Eugene still kept Robert until the day of his death in the year 1974. The ownership was transferred when their house was sold. The new owner, a 10 year old girl, also experienced the same things as Eugene did. 3 decades later and her interviews still insist that Robert is alive and is still trying to kill her.

Now though, Robert is residing in a museum and still continues to taunt visitors with his seem-to-be-changing expression. Guests also relate that taking photos of him without Robert's permission will cause the camera to malfunction.

3. Mandy

Mandy's original owner was unnamed, but it was said that she discovered her in the basement. Reports mentioned that she would hear faint baby cries in the middle of the night and when she inspected the basement, she realized that there was a doll and the window was open.

She decided to donate the doll to a museum, and like

magic, the crying in their home could no longer be heard.

The museum, however, began to experience creepy things.

They noticed that office supplies and personal items kept on going missing. Footsteps could be heard in the museum when no one was there, and lunches disappeared from the refrigerator and would often be found locked in drawers.

And what's more, people who tried to take photos with the said doll suddenly realized that their camera was malfunctioning.

To make matters more interesting, staff related that when Mandy was kept with another doll, it tended to become "jealous", because sooner or later, the other doll would be harmed.

They tried to rectify the situation by placing her alone in a room. It seemed like Mandy did not like to be just by herself so she threw a tantrum by scattering papers all around the room.

There is no clear "legend" to explain how the doll became haunted. One story said that a little girl died in the basement together with her doll. Her spirit became trapped with it and she started mingling with people by scaring them.

There are no evidences to prove this theory though, but the lack of history does no stop people from visiting her in the museum.

Chapter 3 : Horror Movies That Were Based On Real Life Events

There is always something fascinating about real-life movies. One can say that a story has become immortalized, almost similar for when the memories have been published in a book, only this time; things are better… more visual.

But what if the life story being portrayed is not something you want to relive? What if it's not about an ambition achieved, or a love story fulfilled? What if there are horrors lingering… would you dare watch it?

1. Amityville Horror Movie (2005)

The Amityville Horror Movie is perhaps one of the films that set the stage to bring out more true to life horror movies.

Set in 1975, the movie focuses on one family who transferred to a new home in Amityville, New York. Before they bought the house, their broker told them of its history: approximately a year ago, Ronad DeFeo murdered six of his family members in the house.

The broker asked them if it would change their mind

about buying the house, but the couple, thinking that there was nothing wrong about it, pursued the purchase.

They were advised by a friend to bless the house, especially with its murderous history. The priest arrived and when he arrived in a room on the second floor, he heard a male voice telling him to "Get out." He did not mention it to Kathy and George at that time but he did warn them to stay away from that room.

The priest reported to develop a fever and blisters after leaving the house.

Just like anything, they started out well, until the youngest child mentioned that she had a friend named Jodie. Apparently, Jodie was a child of Ronald DeFeo, a child whom he murdered and locked in a closet.

Not only that, but Kathy started to have vivid nightmares of the murders. She started learning who in the family died first and in what room, even though she did zero research on the murders.

From there, things started to go downhill.

George, the head of the family, started to become abusive to the children. He also always strangely woke up at 3:15 am-- the approximate time of the DeFeo murders. When his wife, Kathy-- who was convinced that it was the doing of the house's horror-- tried to evacuate the family out of the house, George attacked her. Fortunately, she was able to knock him out, thus, the spirit who possessed him was driven away.

The ending was realistic though, the family left the house, without even returning for their personal things.

2. The Exorcist (1973)

The film is about a child, Regan, who killed her baby sister and another man (a man whom her mother had a crush on) because she was being possessed. It all started when Regan played with a Ouija board, after that, she started to act strangely-- using bad language, being uncommonly strong, and making scary, mysterious noises.

When it was confirmed that Regan was indeed being possessed by a demon, two priests were called to do the exorcism. One of them, apparently, was already able to defeat the same demon before.

While the exorcism was happening, one of the priests was sent out because he was having trouble concentrating due to the demon's mocking. When he returned, the other priest had already died.

He begged the demon to possess him instead of the child, and when his request was granted, he jumped out of the window as a form of self sacrifice - ultimately completing the exorcism.

According to the author, the facts are based on a 1949 exorcism done in Cottage Maryland. The real story was about a boy who also started acting strangely and was soon sent to be exorcised.

3. Audrey Rose

Audrey Rose is about Ivy who was possessed by a girl named Audrey Rose. Unlike other possession movies, Audrey Rose wasn't evil - in fact, the author centers the movies on reincarnation, rather than possession.

Audrey Rose apparently died in a car accident 2 minutes before Ivy was born. Audrey Rose's father, Hoover, began stalking the family because it had come to his knowledge that his daughter was alive again, in Ivy's body.

When Ivy started acting strangely, only Hoover could calm her down by calling her by her Audrey Rose name. He also explained about the process of reincarnation, but Ivy's parents (more particularly her father) refused to believe him.

In the end, to prove that Ivy was not the reincarnation of anyone else's child, her father urged hypnosis. In the process, Ivy relived the car accident and she died in the traumatic process, prompting the father to believe about reincarnation once and for all.

The author said that this story is based on his own son - whom he heard playing the piano beautifully and perfectly, even when he did not take any piano lessons in the past.

When he consulted an occultist, he said that his son experienced a "reincarnation leak" and that he had already lived numerous lives.

Jo Lavine

Chapter 4 : Spookiest Places Around The World

Going from one place to another is an exhilarating experience-- it lets you meet new people, study new culture, and bask in the views. But what if it can also bring you new horrors? Would you dare visit the spookiest places around the world?

1. Lizzie Borden Bread and Breakfast Museum (United States)

Image Courtesy: David

Would you dare stay the night in the crime scene to an unsolved homicide? If you're brave enough, you can surely be the guest to Lizzie Borden Bread and Breakfast Museum in Fall River Massachusetts.

True Ghost Stories

In the home, which is now a museum, you can book a night of terror, well, depending on your bravery. Allegedly, in 1892, Lizzie Borden killed both her father and her step mother using a hatchet.

Here's the full story;

Mr. Borden was a wealthy man, but despite that, he kept insisting that they had to live frugally. Them being, him, his two daughters, Emma and Lizzie and his second wife, Abby.

According to reports, the family would often eat spoiled food because Mr. Borden did not want to waste any. Abby did not have a good relationship with her husband and her two daughters, who also disliked her. To make matters worse, a man named William visited them to tell Mr. Borden that he was, in fact, his son.

Mr. Borden, of course, rejected it. He even changed his will, and said that his wealth would either go to Abby and her family or all of it was to be donated to charity. That meant no inheritance for Emma, Lizzie and the supposedly illegitimate son, William.

On the morning of August 14, Lizzie, Abby and their maid, Maggie were in the house. Abby went up to arrange things for a guest when the killer opened her window and killed her with a hatchet.

In total, Abby received 19 blows. When Mr. Borden returned, he sat on the couch and the murderer struck him with the same hatchet. This time, the murderer gave him 11 blows.

Due to the number of blows, police concluded that it was a crime of passion-- someone obviously hated the couple and he or she made it known by killing them with such violence. At first, they suspected Lizzie and she was even arrested for it. But since there was a significant lack of evidence, she was also released.

In the museum, you can find photos of the crime scene, and guests often find it terrifying. But, who wouldn't? After all you will be thrown back in time when 2 people were killed and up to now the mystery behind it is still unsolved.

2. Monte Cristo Homestead (Australia)

This building was built in 1885 and since then it has witnessed some of the most terrifying events a family could experience. There was a child whose demise was prompted when he fell down the stairs. A woman fell from the balcony, and a boy who was healthy in all aspects, was burnt to a crisp.

Another spooky story about the Homestead is about a

man who was chained in the Caretaker's Cottage, and beside him lay the lifeless body of his mother. Allegedly, the man was tied there for 40 years.

By 1948, the ownership was transferred and so has the terror. One of the caretakers was murdered right inside the Caretaker's Cottage.

3. The Haunted Vicarage (Sweden)

The Old Vicarage, now known to many as The Haunted Vicarage is a house in Northern Sweden. Although it was built in 1876, the first recorded paranormal activity happened only in 1927 when Nils Hedlund, a chaplain, had witnessed his laundry being thrown haphazardly with sheer yet invisible force.

A priest also saw a woman walking around the house and when he followed her, she promptly disappeared right before his eyes.

Another woman who slept in the guest room reported that she was awakened by 3 women who were looking at her. When she turned on the light, the women were still looking, but the vision became blurry.

Another chaplain recounted that he was thrown out of a chair, again, by an invisible force.

To date, this house is a restaurant slash guest house. Should you be brave enough to stay there for a whole night, the caretakers will give you a certificate - a testament of your bravery!

4. Lawang Sewu (Indonesia)

Image Courtesy: badroe zaman

Headless spirits and a lady who keeps showing up, if you are looking for this kind of thrill - then Lawang Sewu is the place for you.

Built in 1917, Lawang Sewu, literally meaning Thousand Doors, has been witness to many tragic deaths due to the fact that during the Japanese occupation, a lot of people were executed in the basement. A lot of Indonesians were also killed during a battle.

This building is proclaimed as one of the scariest places in Indonesia, where paranormal activities are often caught on tape.

5. Island of Dolls (Mexico)

Image Courtesy: Kevin

It should fascinate anyone to visit a place full of dolls; just imagine how much it will please you to see an island where trees and fences are adorned by these toys! The thing that makes it spooky is the condition of the dolls-- almost all of them are mutilated.

The story started with Don Julian Santana, who together with his small family, lived on the island in the 1950s. Allegedly, when he came there, the ghost of a little girl talked to him-- telling him the story of how she died, by drowning, and of how lonely she was feeling.

To please the girl, Don Julian started collecting dolls and he displayed them on the trees.

Others speculate that it was more than just pleasing the girl, it was to keep the island from her evil grasps. When the spirit still seemed to be displeased, Don Julian garnered even more dolls, even to the point of trading his fruits and vegetables for them.

He also confided to one of his family members that the little girl seemed to want him where she currently was. And apparently, the girl got what she wanted because in 2001, Don Julian drowned, in the same area where the girl was found.

6. Old Changi Hospital (Singapore)

As they say, the darker the history a place has, the more horror it holds. The principle applies to the Old Changi Hospital in Singapore. To think that unlike other haunted structures, Old Changi was just built in 1935.

However, during the Japanese occupation, it was used as a police base, where tortures happened and people were killed. After WWII, it was again used as a hospital until 1997, when the Changi General Hospital replaced it.

The building is now unoccupied and is decaying, but the horrors are withstanding. In fact, several films were shot in the abandoned building, and people often report apparitions of patients and Japanese soldiers.

7. The Belcourt Castle

Image Courtesy: Josh McGinn

The Belcourt Castle is located in Newport, Rhode Island. Aside from its magnificent design, people are also attracted to the lush greens and the tall trees surrounding it.

From 1891 to 1894, the castle was built from the ground up using the expert design of Richard Hunt, a man considered as a pioneer in architecture. Although it was originally made as a summer house, tourists now come and visit the area anytime of the year, what with its appealing vista and relaxing ambiance.

Of course, it also helps that the castle is reported to be a haunted location.

The first owner of the castle was Oliver Belmont, an avid collector of not just armor suits but of manuscripts written way back in the medieval times. From his work in congress and his mighty inheritance from his rich family--

this man had more money than he knew what to do with, and hence, his desire for a luxurious castle.

By the time of its construction, Oliver was still a bachelor, but he soon married a woman named Alva Venderbilt in 1896 and the couple resided in the newly built summer retreat, with Alva making it even more eccentric in style.

Unknown to many, their marriage was surrounded with controversy: Alva was apparently the former wife of Oliver's best friend, William Vanderbilt, whom she had three children with. It wasn't clear whether William was aware of his wife's and his best friend's affair, but not much information was dedicated for that.

After Alva and Oliver were married, they lived in luxury, often times traveling and collecting rare items. In 1908, however, Oliver Belmont died, leaving Alva the rightful owner of the Belcourt.

Alva contributed well in society: aside from giving away hefty contributions to hospitals and other health facilities, she made it her mission to bring gender equality to women by actively joining the women suffrage movement (which enforced government to give ladies the freedom to vote); she also pushed for women's rights in government affairs and business ventures-- all these she did to relieve the pain she felt when her beloved husband, Oliver, left her alone.

At the age of 80, however, she passed on, and the house was given to the eldest Belmont child (Oliver's brother).

Now, the castle is owned by the Tinney family, who opened it as a leisure hotel. Throughout the years, guests' report that the former summer retreat is haunted, came pouring in.

For one, Oliver Belmont's collections of armor suits move from one place to another, without human intervention-- they claimed that the suits have a life of their own. One of the suits can also be heard screaming; according to reports, the previous owner of the suit was shot to death by an arrow which hit him in the eye via the visor slit. And of course, there was a mirror in the castle which when you look at, bears no reflection at all!

As of now, ghost tours are also available in the Belcourt, but participants are rarely allowed to take photos-- some of the guests who secretly brought their camera and took pictures showed that several photos featured unexplained orbs.

Paranormal enthusiasts agree that the owners were not the ones haunting the place, but the rare collections of Oliver (especially the armor suits), which probably have stored energy in them.

10. Edgar Allan Poe in the Western Burial Ground

The Old Western Burial Ground is located in Baltimore in Maryland, United States.

Although a lot of people are unfamiliar with this gravesite, it holds the remains of several famous people, such as Edgar Allan Poe, Francis Scott Key's son, President James Buchanan's grandfather, 15 military heroes from the War in the year 1812 as well as the Revolutionary War, and 5 mayors of the city of Baltimore.

According to experts, the reason why the cemetery is almost forgotten was because of the Westminster Hall (formerly Westminster Presbyterian Church) which was built over a huge part of the graveyard.

While it is true that many tombs are still accessible above ground, some of the burial grounds can now only be visited via the catacombs underneath the building. Paranormal enthusiasts agree that it is in those underground catacombs where the spirits manifest.

One of the most entertaining ghosts in the Western Burial Ground is of course, the ghost of Edgar Allan Poe.

According to witnesses, he is often seen every October 7, the day of his death, and when you spot him, he might converse with you. You might also hear a scream from below the grounds-- if you do, then think of the Screaming Skull of Cambridge, Maryland because it is said to be buried there as well.

Authorities have it that the skull, due to its incessant screaming, was bound, gagged and was buried in a cement tomb, but the screams still live on.

Another ghost was that of Leona Wellesly, an asylum patient, who was buried in her straightjacket; if you happen to see a lady in a straightjacket following you while she is laughing, then make no mistake, it's her.

Another enduring mystery in the burial grounds is about the man who is almost always seen every January 19 (Edgar Allan Poe's birthday). The said man wore completely black clothes, including a black fedora hat and a black scarf which covered his face.

His identity is unknown, but if the witnesses' accounts would be taken into consideration, he has been seen visiting the late author's gravesite for the past 5 decades. Each time, he would leave a bottle of cognac and three stems of a rose; at one point, the offerings included an unsigned note which only said: "Edgar, I haven't forgotten you."

Many people suspected that the man who frequented Edgar Allan Poe's grave was Jeff Jerome, the curator of the late author's house in Baltimore, but he insisted that it wasn't him. To prove his case, he invited over 70 people to celebrate Poe's birthday-- midnight of January 19.

They talked about the author, drank wine, and read some of his most remarkable works. An hour into the celebration, the black man was spotted, so the photographer (backed by LIFE Magazine) took a photo using his infrared night vision camera.

True enough, the man appeared in the photo (featured in one of LIFE'S 1990 issues), and the bottle of cognac and roses were present.

Chapter 5 : Most Unexplained Paranormal Activities

Paranormal - something that cannot be explained, something that can chill your spine because you know that whatever is happening now, should not be happening. What would you do if you happened to encounter paranormal activity?

1. The Famous Reincarnation Case of Biya Pathak

Swarnlata Mishra was said to be the reincarnation of a woman who lived 100 miles from her original location. At the age of three, she had been telling people about the life she lived as a woman named Biya Pathak.

When she reached the age of 10, Dr. Ian Stevenson (perhaps the most famous researcher when it comes to reincarnation), accounted that she was already able to pronounce 50 facts about Biya Pathak's family-- even without contacting any one of them.

One of the things that made her father look into the case more was when Swarnlata said that she had two sons and she described where they lived, in the town of Katni. She gave a full description of the house, and even the houses around it.

She said that Biya Pathak died of "pain in the throat" (take note, Swarnlata even gave the full name of the doctor who treated Biya) and that there was an incident when she and her friend attended a wedding and they had difficulty in finding the bathroom.

The most famous account perhaps is when Biya Pathak's husband heard about the said reincarnation. He and his children (along with other unrelated townspeople) went to Swarnlata Mishra's residence and believe it or not, but Swarnlata was able to easily identify one of the kids-- she even called him "Babu" which was his pet nickname for him.

She even told them that the unrelated townspeople were not familiar to her. She also identified her brother, which she called "Babu".

When she faced Biya's husband, she suddenly became shy and she looked at the ground, a very common Indian tradition. She even recounted the story when Biya's husband stole money from the money box-- an event that was only known to Biya and her husband.

She was also able to identify all the family members, despite the family's attempt to trick her. What they did was deny their own identity, so as to "catch" her should she lie, but Swarnlata stood firm in their correct identities.

Throughout the years, Swarnlata grew up and finished college. From time to time she would reminisce and connect with Biya's family, even admitting that sometimes, she wanted to return to her "old" life, but her loyalty to her current family was also undivided.

2. Vampires are real...

Who can resist the idea of sexy vampires falling in love? Apparently, no one. That's why they have dominated the books, movie's, and even news.

ABC's 20/20 created a documentary about people who are known to be real vampires. No, they do not have the fangs, but they love blood as much as real vampires do. According to them, they have a very rare psychological condition that makes them feel that food is not enough to keep them doing the activities needed in their lives. How do they solve that? They drink blood!

How do they do it?

Well, they pick a sterilized scalpel and poke the skin of a willing donor, when the blood oozes out, they can drink straight from the skin. Donors can actually choose which body part is to be cut. Some "vampires" admit that at times they transfer the blood into drinking glasses - just like how you'll drink a normal juice.

Belfazaar Ashaniston, the one who was interviewed, related that he drinks as often as twice a week.

3. Anneliese and Her 76 Exorcisms

We've seen it in the movies and are terrified beyond ourselves - what if it happened in real life?

We'll talk about the famous exorcism of Anneliese Michel. Are you ready for the story?

It began when 16 year old Anneliese suffered from a severe convulsion in 1968. 5 years later, it seemed that the effect of the convulsion was still haunting the family. Anneliese started to act strangely, that is, she would report that she kept on hearing voices, she told them she saw demons, and she would often make demonic faces.

It got worse, because she would start ripping off her clothes, lick her urine, and she also developed intolerance from any religious item-- especially Holy Water. For two years Annelies suffered it all in a mental institution until her family grew tired of the lack of progress.

The family consulted the Catholic Church, and they confirmed that the girl was being possessed by a demon. For ten full months Anneliese went through 76 exorcisms-- sadly, not one of them was successful. Anneliese eventually died of starvation because she refused to eat anything during the whole period.

Was it a severe case of psychosis that psychiatrists were not able to detect and cure, or was there a very strong demonic presence in her body that even the Catholic Church weren't able to drive away?

Chapter 6 : World's Most Famous Haunted Items

We have discussed about haunted dolls, but now we will learn about the most haunted items you don't ever want your hands to get onto. Or maybe if you are looking for the thrill, you might be interested in having them...

1. The Anguished Man

The Anguished Man is a painting of, well, a man who seems to be very anguished. He seems bald, his face, neck, and a portion of his body that is featured in the painting, is red. His mouth is open, as if he is screaming something. Some paintings are like this, so what makes The Anguished Man a haunted item?

The original owner of the painting was Sean Robinson's grandmother. During his childhood, his grandma would often tell him that The Anguished Man was evil, that the painter mixed his own blood in the red paint to finish the artwork. She related that she could hear cryings, and that a shadow man was often seen lurking in their home.

For 25 years, the painting sat in the house's attic - the intent is to lock away the evil in it.

When Sean Robinson inherited it, his family also experienced unexplained events - the cryings, the shadow, and someone who allegedly touched his wife's hair. His son even fell off the stairs for no apparent reason. Eventually, Sean set up a camera to find out if the painting is indeed haunted - what he discovered was spine chilling.

For a total of 8 hours, the painting fell from the wall, the doors were slammed, and smoke seemed to appear out of nowhere.

The painting still resides in Sean's house, but it is now locked in the basement, but he has no plans of selling it.

2. The Chair of Death

The Chair of Death has a notorious history-- one must say that all of them, the deaths, mind you, were accidental, but it would be weird not to be frightened. And when you learn of its history, you might just say that it truly has the power to cast death to the person sitting on it.

Thomas Busby, a convicted criminal, was scheduled to be hanged a day in 1702. His last request was to be served his final meal in his favorite pub. As customary to a person who is facing his death, his wish, of course, was granted. After his meal, he uttered to no one in particular: "May sudden death come upon to anyone who will sit on my chair."

One can think that mere words cannot hold any grudge, but they soon learned that it can.

Soldiers who sat on the chair never returned from the war they fought. Pilots who sat there crashed their planes. One who was just trying to provoke faith faced an untimely death after he fell in a hole. A construction worker fell from a roof. Even the cleaning lady who just accidentally sat on it, apparently died immediately.

The owner, now convinced that evil is now lurking on the chair, locked it in the basement. Unfortunately, a delivery man who was placing items dared to rest on the chair, and he too, faced an early demise that very same day.

Frustrated, the owner just donated it to a museum. So that no one will dare sit on the chair, even through an accident, the staff of the museum displayed it by hanging it on the wall.

3. The Myrtles Plantation Mirror

Mirrors are mysterious - they are often used in several paranormal rituals. Some people believe that a mirror is capable of trapping spirits of people. Well, can they?

Myrtles Plantation is actually a bed and breakfast, and you would not be surprised to know that it is haunted. Reports say that it is the scene of at least 10 murders, and a lot of paranormal activities are occurring since it's establishment - and why not? It has been built on a burial site.

Perhaps the most notorious item, for the guests that is, is the mirror. Guests relate that they often see figures there... lurking. At times they report that child hand prints suddenly become visible. People believe that those figures were of Sara Woodruff and her children.

Sara and her children were poisoned, and at that time, the people around did not manage to cover the mirror. It was an old saying that when there is a death, mirrors should be covered so that the dead's soul will not be trapped - since they failed to do so, they now think that Sara and her kids are haunting the mirror.

4. The Dibbuk Box

The Dibbuk Box is actually just an ordinary wine cabinet. It was even listed as one item being sold on eBay and was bought by Jason Haxton, who later on wrote a book about the haunted box. His book was then used as a reference for the 2012 movie - the Possession.

The Dibbuk Box' story started in 2011, when an antique dealer got it from an auction. When he returned it home, strange events kept on happening, like lights suddenly turning on, and lightbulbs being smashed. He gave the box to his mother, but then his mother suffered from a stroke. In the hospital she spelled out H-A-T-E-G-I-F-T.

He also tried giving it away to other people, but just a few days after they would return it to him. In the end he decided to sell it on eBay, but he was honest enough to recount the complete story.

5. The Goddess of Death

The Goddess of Death isn't really the name of the "cursed" limestone statue which was dug up in Lemb, Cyprus in the year 1878. Not one report can tell you what the statue exactly is, but experts suspected that it was some form of fertility figure created in 3500 BCE as an offering to an unspecified goddess.

Because of this and the fact that it was discovered in Lemb, people have came to call it "The Women from Lemb" -- at least until it became clear that whoever took ownership of the figure would be subjected to an unexpected demise-- then, it's name started to be The Goddess of Death.

The first person who acquired it was Lord Elphont. History wasn't clear about the causes of death, but within just 6 years of having the statue in their home, all 7 members of the Elphont family died.

The next owner was Ivor Menucci, who, like Lord Elphont, suffered an unexplained death together with his entire family in just 4 years. After Ivor, Lord Thompson-Noel took the statue and suffered the same fate-- his entire family also died after just four years.

The last owner was Sir Alan Biverbrook, but surprisingly NOT ALL of his family died: after his wife, his two daughters, and Sir Alan himself died, two of his sons survived. People began to warn them that the statue could be haunted, so the brothers, not wanting to add their names to the "victims" list, donated the statue to Royal Scottish Museum in Edinburgh.

The curse still lived on, however, because the curator of the museum who handled the figure died within a year.

As of today, the statue is still in the Royal Scottish Museum, and no death was ever reported after the curator's. Do you think the curse already played out? Or perhaps, it was just because the figure is safely behind a glass barrier?

Others even tried to explain how the deaths occurred:

some said that it had some sort of illness-causing bacteria, virus, or fungus which resided in the limestone from which the figurine was made.

This idea became even more famous when the case of the excavators back in the 20th century was revisited. The excavators, headed by Lord Carnarvon, all died due to the fungus which inhabited the mummy wrappings of the boy king, Tutankhamen.

After their digging, the men apparently shaved, and in doing so, they opened their pores (via skin cut), which the fungus used to enter their body.

Although the above story is still questionable (especially since Lord Carnarvon's death is pointed to be caused by mosquito bite), no one is going to try to touch the Goddess of Death anymore, unless of course, they are brave enough.

6. The Basano Vase

The little vase which was made of carved silver is said to bring death to anyone who owns it. Its history started in the 15th century, when it was given to a young woman who was getting married in the village of Napoli.

On her wedding night, however, the woman died (some stories said she was murdered) while she was clutching the vase to her chest. From then, the little vessel was passed on from one family member to another, each owner dying from a certain cause.

After years of being handed over, the vase disappeared, although it wasn't clear how (some said it just vanished, while some people reported that a priest kept it, or another person buried it in an unknown location). The only certain thing was, when it was found in 1988, it contained a small parchment paper with a warning: "Beware, this vase brings death".

Whoever rediscovered the vase took the warning lightly, discarded the paper, and brought the vase to an auction, where of course, it was bought by someone at the price of 4 million Lira (equivalent to more than $2000).

That someone, turned out to be a pharmacist who died after just 3 months of owning the vase. The family sold it to a surgeon who refused to believe in curses; just two months later, the surgeon died despite the fact that he was only 37 years old.

After him, the archaeologist who bought it died of an unknown infection, so his family sold the vase again, but because of its reputation, no one dared to buy it. After a while, someone did, but for a much, much lower price.

The new owner perished too, within one month.

Jo Lavine

Devastated, the family threw the vase out of their window where a policeman (who was almost hit) caught it and tried to return it back to the family (along with a violation ticket). The family accepted the ticket, but not the vase.

The unnamed policeman tried to take the vase to several museums, but not one accepted it. In the end, it was suspected that the policeman simply buried it in a coffin, in an undisclosed location, so that no one would ever be bothered (killed) by it again. Hopefully.

Chapter 7 : World's Most Famous Ghosts

If there are famous haunted places all over the world, there are surely famous ghosts! Who are they? Let's find out!

1. President Abraham Lincoln

Everyone knows that Lincoln was assassinated, but not all had the knowledge that the late president might have had a premonition regarding his own demise.

According to stories, the president confided to his cabinet that he dreamt of going into a funeral while wearing white. When he asked one of the attendees about what was happening, the person replied that the "president has been assassinated."

After the assassination, there were a number of reports that claim of Lincoln's ghost, in the white house, of course.

Among the people who testified about seeing his ghosts were Queen Wilhelmina of The Netherlands, First Lady Coolidge, and the funniest among the witnesses, Winston Churchill.

His story mentioned that while getting out of the

bathroom after a shower, he saw the president by the window near the fireplace. He greeted the president by saying "Good evening Mr. President, you seem to have me at a disadvantage."

The president did not respond in words, but he smiled and disappeared into thin air.

2. Kate Morgan

Kate Morgan checked into Hotel Del Coronado on November 24, 1892. Staff of the hotel noted what a beauty she was, but could not help but be worried because at the time of her arrival, she seemed to be extremely weak. People have speculated that she was taking multiple doses of quinine in an attempt to self-abort the baby in her womb whom she did not want.

5 days later after she had checked into the hotel, she was found dead on the steps going to the beach. The cause of death was a bullet inflicted in her head. A gun was nearby. Due to the scenario, the investigation promptly suggested suicide.

After her death, strange events started happening, and guests would often relate seeing lights being flicked on, doors opening even without anyone nearby, and of course, they reported seeing the ghost of Kate Morgan - a pretty woman in Victorian attire.

3. Anne Boleyn

Stories often suggest that ghosts linger in only one place, but not the ghost of Anne Boleyn. Reports often include that her ghost appear in a lot of places in London, in Bickling Hall, Hever Castle, and of course, her most famous place of appearance - the London Tower.

Before we go on, who exactly is Anne Boleyn?

Anne Boleyn was the 2nd wife of King Henry VIII and she is the mother of Queen Elizabeth I. She only served the title of Queen for three years before King Henry allegedly grew tired of her. She was accused of a lot of things - from witchcraft, to adultery incest.

Most historians, however, believe none of them and suggest that they were merely malicious accusations.

On March 19. 1536, Anne Boleyn faced her death. Accounts also relate that during her execution, the executioner eased her by whispering "Where is my sword", when in fact he already had it and had not wanted Anne Boleyn to wait any further for her final breath.

A lot of people who have seen Anne Boleyn's ghost said that she was as pretty as she was before. A beautiful lady

Jo Lavine

wearing a fantastic gown. Others are not so lucky because they have seen her ghost in the state after her execution: a headless lady who holds her head under her arms.

Chapter 8 : Scary Ghost Towns

A "ghost town" is defined as a deserted placed to the point that no people live there any longer (or sometimes there still are, but only a few). Normally, there are really no ghosts in in a ghost town, but people still find them intriguing (and scary) because of the "remains" of the once lively settlement: abandoned houses, leftover clothes, signages, and other traces of life.

The reasons why a town is abandoned varies, but most of the time, it is because of danger-- perhaps there was health hazard, or, it is an accident prone place. At times, people purposely leave a place because a new area opened up, one with more access to better living.

No matter how normal the circumstances that prompted the resident's departure are, a ghost town will still spark a story; most of the time, a haunted one.

The Curse of Dudleytown

Anyone who enters Dudleytown will be punished by law; on top of being arrested due to trespassing or illegal parking, he or she will also have to pay a fine of at least $75.

The above statement is a warning from Connecticut State Police Department, directed to anyone who plans to explore the remains of Dudleytown, which is located in the north-western part of Connecticut, inside the town of Cornwall.

An area concealed in the shadows of three mountains, Dudleytown has been known as a place of mystery: stories not only suggest that there are ghostly presences in the area, but there are also curses. Despite the warnings (official and otherwise), travelers, ghost hunters, and mystery enthusiasts still use what remains of the roads as their trails.

Dudley Town was founded by a man named Thomas Griffis, but it was from the three Dudley Brothers, who settled in town a few years later, where the town took its name.

What did they do to merit the privilege? History says they left a curse.

The Dudley Brothers traced their pedigree to a man named Dudd, a Saxon, who was a former Duke of Mercia. Dudd died in the year 725 A.D., but before his demise, he was able to take possession of a lot in England, which he called Dudd's leigh (leigh is an old English word which means "land").

Back then, too, people had no surnames, but because they needed to make their identities known, they used their occupation as their last names; examples are the surnames Smith and Baker.

If not their occupation, then they would use the land from which they came from, like Dudley, the shortened version of Dudd's leigh, where the Dudley Castle in England now stands.

In other words, the Dudley Brothers' history originally came from England, and so did the curse they brought to the now abandoned town in northwestern Connecticut.

The curse's story began with Edmund Dudley, a man who tried to overthrow King Henry VIII, but was captured; his punishment for treason was beheading. On the day he was executed in 1510, a curse was bestowed upon all the other Dudleys-- it states that each and every one of them, which came from Edmund's parantage, would be "surrounded by horror" forever. And true enough, it happened-- at least to some.

John Dudley, Edmund's son and the 1st Duke of Northumberland, also attempted to dethrone the king by forcing his son, Guilford, to marry Lady Jane Grey, the infamous Nine Day Queen. All three of them, John, Guilford, and even Lady Jane Grey, were executed due to treason.

Because of this, many Dudleys, in the fear of succumbing to the curse, fled England-- one of those who left was William Dudley, whose wife gave birth to William II in 1634, on a ship headed to America.

William II's son, Joseph, who was born in 1674 at Saybrook, Connecticut, would father 12 children, three of whom would reside in Dudleytown: Gideon, Abiel, and Barzillai.

In 1748, three years after Thomas Griffis bought the land, Gideon Dudley procured a portion of it for farming. 5 years on and two of Gideon's brothers, Abiel and Barzillai, also purchased farming land there. A few years after the three brothers comfortably settled in, a certain Martin Dudley also joined the clan.

At this point, since the number of Dudleys was increasing, people came to know the place as Dudleytown, although technically speaking, it wasn't a town, but just a small portion of land inside Cornwall, the actual town. In fact, it never had its own church, market, or school; all these things could be found in Cornwall.

A few more years and other residents who weren't Dudleys came to settle in the place. According to an 1854 map, the peak population of Dudleytown was 26 families.

Although just a small isolated area, the settlement flourished at some point; the place became widely known for timber, iron, and water mills. Despite the fact that farming was difficult (because the entirety of Cornwall was made of rocks), people still flourished.

Hence, it wasn't clear why and how, but things in Dudleytown started to get bothering: there were people who disappeared mysteriously, residents who became insane, and people who died of unknown causes. It was true that, statistically speaking, the deaths were not that alarming, but since Dudleytown was such a small settlement, it was bound to bring questions, which, up to now, are still unanswered.

For instance, in 1774, an epidemic came into the Adoniram Carter household-- the result was tragic: it killed the entire family. The Nathaniel Carters, relatives of the Adoniram Carters, were devastated by the loss, so they moved to Binghamton, New York, where the Indians killed Nathaniel, his wife, and their infant child.

Their three remaining children were kidnapped and were brought to Canada, where the two daughters were ransomed, and the son, David, stayed with his captors, married an Indian girl, and escaped the curse of Dudleytown: he turned to United States to get formal education and later on became a Supreme Court Judge.

Another resident of Dudleytown, General Heman Swift, also experienced the curse; according to stories, in April of 1804, Sarah Faye, the General's wife, was struck by lightning right on their front porch. Immediately after his wife's death, the General was reported to have gone demented.

One more unfortunate man to experience the curse was Horace Greeley, the founder of the *New York Tribune*. According to stories, Horace had married Mary Cheney, a resident of Dudleytown; in 1872, Mary took her own life, and a week after that, Horace lost his bid for presidency.

This story, however, deserves to be untold: the truth is, Mary Cheney was not born in Dudley, nor did she live in the area-- she was, however, from Litchfield, a nearby place. Secondly, she didn't take her own life; Mary died because of a lung disease.

After the Civil War, people began abandoning Dudleytown; it could be because of the curse, which they thought was present, but it could also be because of the place itself. As we have mentioned, Dudley was rocky, so farming couldn't be sustained; moreover, the winter season was harsh.

So was Dudleytown really cursed? Debunkers suggest that it isn't; they explained that people who became demented were already old in age, and so, senility was normal. The deaths could be because of poor health care, and disappearances could have happened voluntarily.

In fact, even Barzillai, Gideon, and Martin, who left the town, lived long and peacefully. It was only Abiel who stayed and became buried in debts; he died at the age of 90 in 1799 and although reports said he was demented before his death, debunkers said financial difficulties could actually drive a person to insanity.

However, no debunker could explain the next unexplained event that we will discuss.

It happened in 1901, when Dudleytown was losing most of its residents; one of the last inhabitants, John Patrick Brophy, happened on perhaps one of the most unfortunate series of events.

First, his wife died of tuberculosis and although that was common during the early 1900s, John's devastation wasn't lessened. Shortly after the funeral, his two daughters vanished in the forests and never returned; people said it was voluntary, especially when the two were accused of stealing, but no proof of intent was found.

Immediately after the mysterious disappearance, the Brophy house was burnt to a crisp-- the cause was never identified. After that, John himself vanished without a trace.

Whatever happened to John Patrick Brophy and his daughters, we might never know, but they became some of Dudleytown's "casualties". By the 1940s, the ghostly stories in the ghost town began, and up to now, still persisted.

Each time someone dares to trespass the area, there would be an account of negative feeling, ghostly touches, disembodied voices, and unexplained lights and sounds. There were even reports of inhumane creatures that caused insanity.

The Silent Hill in Pennsylvania

True Ghost Stories

Image Courtesy of Jo Guldi from Flicker

Silent Hill is a 2006 film about a couple, Rose and Christopher, who experienced some problems with their adopted daughter, Sharon. Because Sharon kept on sleepwalking and whispering the name of the town "Silent Hill", Rose decided to bring her to the town in question.

Once they reached the place, strange events started happening. Sharon disappeared and monsters began attacking. Soon enough they discovered that Silent Hill was once plagued with witch-burning, and that Sharon's other self, was a victim of it.

Believe it or not, but some people think that Silent Hill is real, and that it is Centralia, the ghost town in Columbia County, Pennsylvania.

One could describe Centralia as a hell on earth; below the abandoned lands are (apparent) burning mines, which could get so hot that it would boil ground water enough to release steam, creating the ghost town's foggy appearance. Drive around and you'll notice few living people, instead, you will encounter three cemeteries; in other words, most of the town's residents are the buried dead.

Citizens who have abandoned the place couldn't be blamed; after all, why would they subject themselves to a hellish surrounding when they could comfortably move elsewhere? Soon enough the Zip Code 17927, which was originally assigned for Centralia, was revoked.

The town's appearance often lights up ghostly rumors and paranormal happenings; some say that the dead buried in the three cemeteries are restless in the knowledge that the settlement they had come to love does no longer exist. Their restless souls could be the source of the disembodied voices, spiritual apparitions, and creepy feelings.

Some of the unexplained events were discussed in *Off Roaders*.

First, there was the story of Ruth Edderson, who explored Centralia in 1998 during a fall season. Together with a friend, Ruth saw a couple of people emerge from the hole behind a graveyard-- the people were wearing mining helmets (which was unusual), and after a few moments, they vanished along with the steam which came from the same subsidence hole.

A resident of New Jersey, Scott Sailor, also related a spooky happening, to which his response was to say that "there was something wrong with the place" and that he "isn't coming back".

Scott's tour with his friends started out great-- they saw the famous landmarks in Centralia, like the cracked Rt. 61 and the burning hillside; they witnessed the remains of a ghost town and felt the town it was once. When they reached the eastern part of the town, however, strange things began happening.

It started with just steam coming from a hill, but as they observed the fossils, Scott and two of his friends, heard a voice coming from below the ground. The first sounds were inaudible, and they assumed it was just from some other visitors exploring the place, so they ignored it.

However, the sound was heard again, and this time it was clearer: "leave this place..." (or something along those lines).

At that point, Scott admitted that the hill was becoming steamier and the smell was awful (probably from sulfur), and that since they were already spooked, they headed back to the car. As they left, the voice spoke again and said: "Why... Why did you do that?" Scott was reluctant in telling the story, but still figured that he should share this one.

In 1999, Jim (his surname was not given) and his girlfriend, Laurie, went to the same place and experienced scary things as well. Jim's story opened up by saying that they weren't superstitious people; whenever they could, they would visit abandoned dwellings, old houses, and creepy cemeteries and they would be okay. However, their trip to Centralia "gave them a fright".

Jim mentioned that in the ghost town, there was an abandoned twin home at the side of the street, located at one of the hills. The two units had red numbers displayed on the front, probably an indication that they would be demolished soon. Jim and Laurie noticed that the back door was opened, so in they went and explored the slightly dark house (because the windows were boarded).

Finding nothing of interest on the first floor, they decided to check out the second floor. For a few minutes, everything was okay, but all of a sudden, they heard footsteps coming from the third floor.

Initially, the couple thought that someone else was inside the house, so they just waited-- however, when the sounds became louder (indicating that the person was nearing) and no one emerged from the stairs connecting the second and the third floor, Jim and Laurie decided it was time to go.

According to Jim, it was as if someone was using the stairs but they couldn't see him (or her). Frightened, they made a beeline to the back door, headed to their car, and drove away. When they were brave enough to look back, they were half expecting that someone from the window was watching them-- but there was no one.

Whether or not Centralia is a true Silent Hill, the place has surely left a mark in the lives of several people.

Seattle Underground

Image Courtesy of Doug Kerr from Flickr

Jo Lavine

Image Courtesy of Karen Neoh

Exploring places always brings excitement to people, especially if the destination is filled with memories-- such places are museums that contain various items of importance, and old, preserved streets where you can see the time-worn establishments and houses.

For some people, however, the joy of exploration can be achieved by entering one abandoned place and savoring the feeling that once, there were people there; they laughed, cried, and told stories there, but now, the place is derelict. Of course, if you are a paranormal enthusiast, seeing a ghost would be an added bonus.

Such was the goal of Susan Tredder, when she decided to join Seattle Underground Tours which had the title, *Underground Paranormal Experience*. Susan was accompanied by two friends (whom she promised the tour wouldn't be scary).

After handing over their jackets because the tunnel was

too hot for added garments, they were provided with a vest containing "ghost detecting" equipment which included an EVP recorder (in case there were disembodied voices), and an EMF device to detect energy presence which could come from ghosts.

Before proceeding with the tour, they were asked to watch an episode of *Ghost Hunters*, a show on the Travel Channel. The episode was about the team's encounter when they investigated the Seattle Underground, and since it included "experiences" such as hearing weird knocks and bumps, the participants of the tour visibly became pumped up.

Headed by the tour guide, the participants entered the tunnel one by one. They passed by a locked door and the guide told the story of a murdered man who died violently right in that area; he called to the man, asking for him to make his presence known, but to no avail-- the man didn't grant the guide's request.

There was nothing paranormal that Susan and her friends could detect, but she said the tour in itself was worth it. Does that mean that ghost town in Seattle Underground isn't really haunted?

Not really.

In fact, participants from the other tours claimed that a

lot of paranormal things happened in the tunnels. The experiences included (but were not limited to) sudden feeling of pain and woe, which couldn't be explained. Most of the time, only women participants experience it, and it only happens when they reach an area in the tunnel called "Prostitution Area".

Then, in an Old Bank Vault, some men felt cold breeze (remember it was supposed to be hot inside the tunnels), and a few of them saw an apparition of a miner.

Blog posts about their experience in the Underground were also interesting; one claimed that right after the tour, her camera's batteries died down. She admitted that she took some photos and videos, but claimed that it was still weird because during a vacation, the camera took one week before it needed charging.

On top of that, one of the photos she captured was blurred; while it wasn't weird per se, she insisted that it was the only photo with poor quality. Desiring to at least make it better, she used basic editing, but the quality became even worse.

In the end, she decided that it didn't mean anything, even when the area where the photo was taken was said to be haunted by a white lady.

If the witnesses' accounts would be taken into

consideration, it was clear that the tunnel was haunted, but the question is, how did it become haunted? While Dudleytown and Centralia are areas above ground, how come Seattle Underground was a town beneath the lands?

According to history, Seattle in the 1800s was made largely of woods. Houses, shops, and establishments-- everything was made of fragile lumber-- so when a fire started in 1889 (known as the Great Seattle Fire), it became almost impossible to put it out.

Firefighters used too much water which damaged the city's water pressure, but even with that effort, the fire was able to destroy 26 city blocks. It was then that the City of Seattle decided to rebuild the place, but only if two changes would take place: first, everything should be made with stone or brick, and second, the new city would be established 1-2 stories higher than before.

The first change was because of their trauma of the fire, and the second was due to the frequent occurrence of flood. When the new city was built, many people immediately moved there, except for some (mostly merchants) who opted to stay in the undamaged portion of the now Underground Seattle.

In 1907, however, the City of Seattle "condemned" the tunnels due to the fear of epidemic. And so, the once lively city was literally buried underneath the land and figuratively within the people's mind.

Ghost towns are sad towns-- imagine the fact that people once lived there; they walked, shared stories, gossiped, and worked in the area, and now, the place they once knew is no more. Perhaps, the reason why ghost towns are haunted is because of the memories, which experts agree, leave an imprint that can manifest in the world of the living.

Chapter 9 : Bizarre Creatures

Although bizarre creatures are no longer a thing now, since technological advancement and sciences have debunked many legends, there still are cases which could not be explained. Two such cases are the Beast of Croglin Grange, a vampire, and the Hairy Hands of Dartmoor United Kingdom.

The Beast of Croglin Grange was a one-time experience for a woman named Amelia Cranswell, but the tale of the Hairy Hands still plagued Dartmoor, constantly bringing fear to the motorist whenever they reach a certain road after sunset.

The Vampire of Croglin Grange

Vampires have been a part of our culture for so long; before, they were pictured as the blood-sucking, cape-wearing men, who sucked the blood out of someone's neck at the dead of the night, and then, after their "meal", they would turn into bats.

The origin of vampires is vague, but the reality that they became a sold-out phenomenon in Eastern Europe (particularly in Bulgaria, Serbia, Romania, and the Slavic people of Russia), cannot be disputed. In fact, between the 11th and the 18th century, many "vampire hysteria" cases happened in those areas-- they believed that some local deaths were caused by vampires.

Now, the concept of vampires has evolved-- they are now viewed as people who can communicate with us in broad daylight; they are individuals who have come back from the dead, and now have the power to live immortally.

With the vampires' evolution... one can't help but wonder: are vampires real? For the English people, these creatures were non-existent until the 18th century, when the Vampire of Croglin Grange made a name for itself.

Stories have it that Croglin Grange was a stone-dwelling in Cumberland, England and that the Fisher Family had owned it for centuries; however, in the 1800s, they decided to move into a much bigger space (the Croglin Grange was only one-story), so they looked for people who would rent or lease it.

However, the process of letting it took time, in fact, the entire winter-- so in that period, the Croglin Grange sat empty. In the spring though, the Cranswell siblings (2 brothers, Michael and Edward, and 1 sister, Amelia) became interested in the dwelling, so the Fisher Family rented it out to them.

Everything was going smoothly-- the trio adjusted well to the neighborhood and they seemed to love their new home, until one summer night...

On that hot day, Amelia told her brothers that she would be retiring to bed early because she wasn't feeling well; when she reached her room, she proceeded to close the windows, when suddenly, from the churchyard (which was visible from her room), she saw two moving lights that seemed to approach their house.

Slightly scared, but still not wanting to be too superstitious, she bolted the windows, went to bed, and fell asleep. However, she woke up when something rustled from outside-- Amelia got up from bed and with sheer horror, she noticed that a creature, with corpse-like hands, was trying to remove the bolts of her window, and was succeeding.

When the last of the lead was detached, Amelia was already too terrified to scream, and worse, she couldn't even breathe. In one swift motion, the humanoid creature approached her -- it's face deathly, it's lips and eyes bright red -- it grabbed her hair and pulled her close as if it would deliver a kiss.

Only, it didn't, for it bit her throat.

The noise of the commotion and her blood curdling

scream woke her brothers, who rushed and opened her doors by smashing it with a poker. One of them tended to Amelia, who was bloodied, while the other tried to chase the culprit, but it was too late... it already had escaped.

They summoned a doctor, and after hours of treatment, Amelia survived. Thinking that it was a traumatic ordeal, the physician advised the siblings to have a vacation once Amelia was fit to travel. And so, off they went to Switzerland where Amelia recovered.

Unlike the modern tales about vampires that we have now, where a person who is bitten would turn into a vampire, no accounts in the Croglin Grange tales mentioned that Amelia turned; she had a near death experience, but she survived and remained human.

Her brothers, however, couldn't get over the fact that someone tried to kill their sister, so Michael and Edward promised that they would seek revenge. Hearing this, Amelia offered to be their bait, and despite their disapproval, the two protective brothers, relented.

So in their return during the winter season, Amelia stayed vigil while her brothers lurked in the shadows; when the creature, for the second time, succeeded to remove the bolts, Michael and Edward rushed to the scene and shot at it.

Surprised, the beast of Croglin Grange immediately went back to the direction it came from, and even though Michael and Edward wanted nothing more than to follow it, they knew that it would be dangerous, so they waited for daybreak.

As the first rays of light shone, the Cranswell brothers, along with many residents, started to their conquest: they searched the surrounding area to see if something was amiss, finding none, they concentrated on the nearby church.

In it, they also saw nothing wrong, until one of the men noticed that the door to the crypt was slightly ajar. While they expected coffins and sarcophagi in the crypt, they were horrified by the scene presented in front of them: all around the crypt where ruined coffins and human bone fragments, but there in one corner, was a coffin which withstood whatever storm had happened.

Slowly, the men approached the sole coffin and opened it; there inside was a man, with an almost translucent skin and cold eyes-- one of his legs was sporting a fresh pistol wound.

Astounded, the residents could only drag the coffin out and burn it together with its demonic content.

To date, no one could surmise why the Beast of Croglin

Grange awakened during the Cranswells' stay, when it didn't disturb the Fisher Family in their centuries of residence there. Perhaps, its dereliction during the whole season of winter triggered something sinister... or maybe it was just the first time someone survived the ordeal.

While a lot of people tried to debunk the story, defending that there was not such place as Croglin Grange, the people of England still considered this a legend.

The Hairy Hands of Dartmoor

The Hairy Hands of Dartmoor, like the Beast of Croglin Grange, also originated in England. In what is known today as the B3212 road, one that is between the Two Bridges and Postbridge, a horrifying tale took place.

According to stories, during the early 1900s (some reports said it began in 1910), road users in that area of Dartmoor would be disturb by hairy hands which appeared out of nowhere. The hands would take control of the wheel, steering your vehicle to the wrong direction, and no matter how much you tried to get it right back on track, you simply weren't strong enough..

In the early 1900s, a series of road accidents plagued Dartmoor, but the people were not worried; after all, based from the reports of those who experienced the horror of the hairy hands, the phenomenon seemed harmless; the worst that could happen to you was be nervous, be late, or be steered away from the right direction. However, the complacence of the community was shaken in the year 1921.

In June of that year, Dr. E.H. Helby (a prison doctor) was driving home; he was manning the motorcycle while his two children stayed in the side-car. All of a sudden, Dr. Helby lost control of the vehicle -- it happened so fast -- after commanding his children to jump out to safety (which they were able to do), the doctor was thrown out of his vehicle and died a swift death.

While Dr. Helby didn't live to tell the story of how he lost control of his vehicle, a British Army Captain was able to. It was in August 26, 1921, when the said captain, who, according to many people, was an experienced rider, also lost control of his motorcycle in the same road that took Dr. Helby's life.

According to the captain, it wasn't his fault: "Believe it or not, but something drove me off the road," he said during one of his interviews. He swore that out of thin air, a pair of muscular, hairy hands, closed over his and started directing the vehicle; he added that he gave it all his strength, but he was weak compared to the severed, monstrous hands.

Since then, several more motorists have been unfortunate to meet the Hairy Hands of Dartmoor, one of them was Theo Brown, a famous folklorist from Devonshire who penned *Family Holidays Around Dartmoor* and *Devon Ghosts*.

In the summer of 1924, she, along with her husband, were campaigning on the famous road, when suddenly, a pair of hairy hands crept towards them. According to Theo, she knew right away that those hands were evil-- that no amount of fighting would save them from it.

She felt that it hated them and wished them harm, so immediately, she made a Sign of the Cross and offered a prayer for their safety. Slowly, the hands creeped away from them, and Theo said another prayer of thanks.

Perhaps the hands were truly evil in nature and weren't just playing around? The fact that it disappeared at the Sign of the Cross was a dead give away. In fact, in the 1920s, a woman, who was sleeping in a caravan experienced the same thing: she saw the hands approaching the window, so she offered a prayer and a Sign of the Cross-- the hands then slowly vanished.

Did the government not do anything about it? They did.

Truth was, when the *Daily Mail* picked up on the issue, it became highly publicized that the local government opted to act: they sent some engineers to inspect the roads; they figured that perhaps, the road needed repairs. Despite the repairs, the tale of the Hairy Hands still continued, even to this day.

If you happen to reach Dartmoor and the infamous B3212 Road, heed the warnings: no matter what time of the day it is, and no matter what kind of vehicle you are driving, be careful.

Offer a short, sincere prayer in advance and ask for protection. Of course, there is a chance that you won't believe any of the accounts we have listed here, but being careful on the road is always a prerequisite -- so, grip for control...

Chapter 10 : Hotel Mysteries

Most hotel experiences are great: abundant food, accommodating staffs, top notched facilities, and comfortable bed... but what if the hotel you are staying at is plagued with mystery? Will you check out the next morning, or would you find it more exciting?

1. The Haunting in Bitmore Hotel

The Bitmore Hotel can be found in downtown Miami in Florida, particularly in Coral Gables. Throughout the years, its old world beauty has charmed the local, national, and international society, but even though it looks elegant and classy, several people who have checked in there attest that the hotel is haunted.

Like many other haunted establishments, the Bitmore had a long history-- the building was established in 1926 (by George Merrick, the known founder of Coral Gables) and in an instant, it had been the talk of the town; one after the other, events took place there, most of them were fashion shows, galas, golf tournaments, and extravagant parties.

When the 1940s came, the Bitmore Hotel was turned into

a military hospital until 1973, when the Historic Monuments Act let the Coral Gables take ownership of it. However, since the grand establishment was in great need of repairs and refurbishing, no further action followed; hence, the building stood abandoned for another ten years.

In 1983, the city of Coral Gables decided that it was time to restore its charm, so they shelled out a large sum of money to turn the old building into a deluxe hotel once more.

The process took about 4 years, but it was worth it -- the Bitmore opened again in 1987. Still, the people thought it needed more extravagance, forcing the state to spend another 18 million dollars to make it stand out. Only then did the private hotel organization take notice of the Bitmore-- they requested to take over and they succeeded. As a response, they spent another $40 million for major improvements.

Even with the amount of money used to erase the old traces of the once derelict hotel, the hauntings still happened. The fact that it was a hospital before meant that many people (mostly veterans) died in the place-- they are said to still be on duty.

Another story said that there was a mother who died in

the Bitmore in an attempt to save her three year old son, who climbed to the balcony of their high-rise suite; now, people believed she was haunting that particular suite.

Paranormal experts agree that such events could lead to haunting; according to them, if a person died while trying to save a loved one, he or she may linger in the place because of the lack of knowledge if the loved one had been saved or not.

In March 4, 1929, one gangster, Thomas "Fatty" Walsh, was shot to death by the hotel manager, Eddie Wilson. The murder happened in the former casino, on the 13th floor, and although there were witnesses, Eddie was never punished, in fact, because he allegedly had some strong connections, he was able to escape to Cuba, unscathed.

Because Fatty loved his gangster life so much (the women, extravagant living, and highly profitable businesses), and because his life was taken all of a sudden, his haunting, according to many paranormal experts, was expected-- people like him were not prepared to "cross-over" yet, so they stay.

Guests of the Bitmore said that the entire 13th floor was haunted; there was one instance when a couple was taken to the 13th floor even though it wasn't their intended destination-- when the girl stepped out, the elevator doors closed and the man was brought down to the lobby. Could it be Fatty Walsh's ghost?

Some said yes, because he allegedly loved women, especially attractive ones. Once the girl was left alone, she would immediately feel a presence, smell a cigar, and hear a chuckle. When former president Bill Clinton stayed in one of the 13th floor suites, he interestingly experienced the haunting: while watching a game on the television, it suddenly turned off, and then after a few moments, it turned on again.

Bothered (and perhaps a little annoyed), he called the staff and they tried to see what was wrong with the TV, but couldn't find any-- still, it continued to turn on and off.

During the 10 years of the hotel's dereliction, people who stood at the golf course behind the hotel noticed a couple of disturbing things, such as opening and closing of windows and flickering lights. No one thought of it as paranormal in nature, in fact, the people were worried that transients were already taking over the place so they called the local authorities.

Police agreed with their assumption and headed out to the abandoned Bitmore, but upon entering, they saw no drifters, however, they witnessed several unexplained apparitions, they heard glasses breaking and disembodied voices; even the dogs which they brought ran out of the hotel because of fear.

Although it is a little disconcerting at first, the presence of the ghosts at the Bitmore now serves like an attraction, especially the ghost of Fatty Walsh who seems to like the company and the attention.

His apparitions are mostly seen in bathroom mirrors, and believe it or not, but guests even saw an invisible finger writing the word "BOO!" in the mirrors. In the 1970s, a séance was performed on the 13th floor of the hotel, and as expected, Fatty Walsh talked to the participants-- he even related the story of how he died. As the people from the séance toured the Bitmore, Fatty was following them-- as if he was the host!

If one time you choose to visit the Bitmore, would you welcome Fatty's presence? He sure will welcome yours!

2. Banff Springs Hotel (Canada)

Luxurious interiors and scenic views, but do not be fooled. Banff Springs Hotel in Alberta, Canada is believed to be one of the most haunted hotels in the country.

Reports always point to three paranormal happenings.

The first is about the family who was murdered in room 873. Since the murder, the door of the room has been bricked up, but that did not stop the family from appearing to guests, often just outside the same room, or in the hallways.

And who can forget the dashing bride? It was retold that there was once a bride who died in the stairwells. She was supposed to come down, romantically, with candles lighting her path down the stairs.

Unfortunately, her wedding gown caught fire and in a panic, she fell down - breaking her neck in the process. Guests would often report that they see a bride in full wedding gown in the ballroom, dancing.

And of course, there is the Phantom Bellboy. Sam Macauley worked in the Banff Springs from the 1960s to 1970s. Apparently, he loved the job that even after death he is still serving guests.

Reports say that he will often show the guests to their rooms unlock it and help them carry their baggage. Try to talk to him or try to give him a tip, and he will vanish right before your eyes.

3. The Savoy Hotel in Mussoorie, Uttarakhand (India)

The Savoy Hotel is a building of luxury, then and now: it was built using English Gothic Architectural style which became prominent between the 12th and 15th century AD and its grounds measures up to 11 acres. The majestic beauty of the place, along with its historic appeal, makes it one of the most sought after hotels in India.

However, some stories also mention that the hotel is haunted.

According to history, Mussoorie, the place where the hotel was built, became popular as the "Pleasure Capital" in the early 1900s, especially for British people who wanted to enjoy the summer season.

This gave Cecil D. Lincoln, an Irishman barrister, the idea of a hotel, so in 1895, after owning the Rev. Maddock's Mussoorie School and demolishing it, he began building The Savoy. After 5 years, the Savoy Hotel was completed, but since it still needed furbishing, it opened to the public in 1902 (apparently, since there were no roads, the only way to carry heavy furniture pieces uphill was through bullock carts).

Back then, there were two other successful hotels: The Cecil at Simla, and The Carlton at Lucknow, but in 1906, the Princess of Wales (who would be the future Queen Mary) chose to stay at The Savoy and in doing so, made the hotel famous.

However, shortly after the princess left, a massive earthquake erupted which ruined most of the hotel's structures. For one full year it was closed down and was opened again in the year 1907. The popularity of The Savoy didn't dwindle, in fact, in 1909, when the hotel started using electricity, it became even more luxurious and famous.

From then on, many celebrities and royalties frequented the historic Savoy, ranging from princes to dignitaries and Nobel Prize awardees.

In 1911, however, things started to become even more "exciting" at the arrival of Miss Frances Garnett-Orme, a 49 year old woman who was accompanied by Miss Eva Mountstephen. According to reports, Miss Frances was engaged to a British officer, but before the marriage, her fiancé died-- for an unknown reason, she was left with a psychic ability after that loss.

Together with Miss Eva, Miss Frances became an expert in performing séances and crystal reading. After a few days of staying in The Savoy, Miss Eva left for Lucknow while Miss Frances decided to stay at the hotel.

Then the unthinkable happened: Miss Frances was found dead in her room a few days later.

From the police's point of view, it was clearly murder, despite the fact that her room was locked from the inside. A post mortem examination revealed that the 49 year old died due to prussic acid poisoning, a hydrogen cyanide which is a colorless liquid.

A few months after the investigation took place, Miss Frances' doctor was also found dead due to strychnine ingestion (a highly poisonous pesticide).

The Police arrested Miss Eva due to the suspicion that she mixed the prussic acid in Miss Frances' bottle of sodium bicarbonate (her medicine), but of course, due to the lack of evidence, the court had to release her. People, however, believed that Miss Eva used her psychic ability from afar to "force" Miss Frances to mix the poison and drink it. Up to now, Miss Frances' death is still unsolved.

The mystery around it encouraged renowned author, Agatha Christie, to write a book featuring the story, it is entitled: The Mysterious Affair at Styles.

Today, guests at the hotel reported seeing a floating silhouette of a woman in the halls, toilets flush without human intervention, and whispers can be heard. At one point, they were even able to record a woman singing. The tell-tale signs of paranormal activity such as doors opening, lights switching on and off, and items getting lost and found are also present.

As luxurious as it is, The Savoy Hotel, with its history and Miss Frances' death, is really bound to be filled with memories, if not ghosts.

Conclusion

From now on, I'm sure you will be careful with the places you go to, and especially the items you buy. From time to time, remember to research about an object's history before purchasing it.

Paranormal activities and ghosts in general will continue to fascinate the minds of people. It is in our nature to be drawn to something that cannot be explained. It urges the wheels of our minds to work. Whatever you decide to do after reading this book, one thing remains to be certain, you have to be careful.

Thank you again for purchasing this book, and congratulations on finishing a spine-chilling journey!

If you enjoyed this book, do you think you could leave me a review on Amazon? Just search for this title and my name on Amazon to find it. Thank you so much, it is very much appreciated!

Do you want more books?

How would you like books arriving in your inbox each week?

They're FREE!

We publish books on all sorts of non-fiction niches and send them to our subscribers each week to spread the love.

All you have to do is sign up and you're good to go!

Just go to the link below, sign up, sit back and wait for your book downloads to arrive.

We couldn't have made it any easier. Enjoy!

www.LibraryBugs.com

Links to photos

Robert the doll -

https://www.flickr.com/photos/cayobo/6009133523/

Lizzie Borden house -

https://www.flickr.com/photos/bootbearwdc/3535957840/

Lawang Sewu -

https://www.flickr.com/photos/gadulz/13318151705/

Island of dolls -

https://www.flickr.com/photos/kevin53/15728653751/

Belcourt castle -

https://www.flickr.com/photos/svenstorm/3783171269/

Centralia -

https://www.flickr.com/photos/landschaft/4993954485/

Centralia -

https://www.flickr.com/photos/landschaft/4993953595/

Underground Seattle -

https://www.flickr.com/photos/dougtone/6015177232/

Underground Seattle -

https://www.flickr.com/photos/kneoh/5088624704/

Printed in Great Britain
by Amazon